WILEY & GRAMPA'S CREATURE FEATURES

NIGHT OF THE LIVING EGG NOG

WRITTEN AND ILLUSTRATED BY

KIRK SCROGGS

TERROR YOU CAN TASTE, CHILLS YOU CAN CHUG!

LITTLE, BROWN AND COMPANY
Books for Young Readers
New York   Boston

This book is in loving memory of Betty Aulds.

———————

Special Thanks to:
Steve Deline, Jackie Greed, Suppasak Viboonlarp, Mark Mayes,
Hiland Hall, Amy Pennington, Alejandra, Inge Govaerts, Joe Kocian,
Jim Jeong, Will Keightly, Mrs. Nelson's Books, Tim Nelson, and the
mezz crew woo woo!

A special holiday-spiced thanks to Andrea, Jill, Alison, Elizabeth,
Saho, Sangeeta and the Little Brown crew.

An extra noggy thanks to Ashley & Carolyn Grayson and Dav Pilkey.

And a super, nutmeg-sprinkled thanks to Harold Aulds and
Diane and Corey Scroggs.

Little, Brown and Company

Hachette Book Group USA
237 Park Avenue, New York, NY 10017
Visit our Web site at www.lb-kids.com

First Edition: October 2007

ISBN-13: 978-0-316-00685-9 / ISBN-10: 0-316-00685-8

10 9 8 7 6 5 4 3 2 1

WOR

Printed in the United States of America

Series design by Saho Fujii

The illustrations for this book were done in Staedtler ink on Canson Marker paper,
then digitized with Adobe Photoshop for color and shade.
The text was set in Humana Sans Light and the display type was handlettered.

CHAPTERS

CHAPTER 1

Thick and Creamy

Ladies and gentlemen...I'd like to take a moment to talk about eggnog. To some, eggnog is a delicious holiday beverage that brings joy to all. To the rest of us sane and normal folks, it is a disgusting yellow milky concoction that resembles elephant mucus.

This is a heartwarming story about eggnog—rivers of evil, frothy, putrid eggnog. So sit down, dim the lights, and pour yourself a big ol' glass. Enjoy.

Look out! A stream of eggnog is headed straight for you!

No, wait! That's just Jubal demonstrating his awesome ability to shoot milk out of his nose. It was only a few days until Christmas vacation and Jubal was celebrating with a twenty-one-nostril salute.

REHEARSAL
TODAY AT 3:00
CHRISTMAS
MUSICAL
JINGLE
BELL
STOMP

TOXIC

MAD
SCIENCE
MADE EASY

"Hey! Watch it!" I yelled. "You almost hit my science project. I've spent weeks perfecting my Superblob 3.5 formula."

"Do you really think it's a good idea to have such dangerous chemicals in the cafeteria?" asked Jubal.

"Yeah," said Coach Haunch. "You wouldn't want to contaminate those perfectly good toxic chemicals with Vera's cooking."

"This is no ordinary batch of toxic chemicals,"
I said. "It can be sculpted into any form."

"Hey! It's Santa!"
said little Mary Ann.

"Or it can be used for
educational purposes.
Just look at this sculpture
of our nation's capitol...

or this authentic baboon's butt."

"Neato!" said Mary Ann. "It jiggles just like the
real thing!"

Suddenly, we heard a shriek from the kitchen! It was Vera, fresh back from her vacation and out of her mind.

"Help! Help!" she screamed. "Something slimy and horrible just attacked me in the kitchen!"

"Are you sure it wasn't the Salisbury steak with brown gravy?" I asked.

"Nooo!" she screamed. "This was much more vicious!"

CHAPTER 2

The Kitchen Stink

We gathered whatever weapons we could find and bravely crept into the kitchen. The air was filled with the smell of rot and doom, which was, of course, perfectly normal.

"You guys go ahead without me," said Coach Haunch nervously. "I'm gonna go check on the parking lot and make sure our precious fleet of school buses is okay."

"Whatever it is, it's in the fridge," said Vera.

We approached the refrigerator with caution. It was vibrating, and strange fluids were leaking out of it—again, perfectly normal.

We opened the door to find...

"Argh! A monster!" I screamed.

"Don't be frightened," said Vera. "That's just my holiday meat loaf snowman. I made it myself from seven different types of meat."

CHAPTER 3

E.T.—The Eggy Tentacle

"Sorry, Vera," I said. "It'll have to be removed and destroyed. We can't take any chances. In fact, just to be safe, I think we should seal this whole area off and destroy every bit of food in this kitchen."

Just then, a slimy tentacle slithered out of the fridge and tapped Jubal on the shoulder!

The tentacle came from a rancid carton of eggnog in the back of the fridge.

"Good gravy!" I yelled. "Vera, that carton of eggnog expired in 1983! It's so rotten, it's come to life!"

"Well, I was saving it for a special occasion," said Vera.

Suddenly, the carton of eggnog jumped out of the fridge and spit a stream of expired nog right at our heads.

"This little guy's got some impressive moves!" said Jubal.

"Look!" I screamed. "The carton is hopping toward the lunchroom. We can't let it escape. Stop that beverage!"

CHAPTER 4

What About Blob?

The kids in the cafeteria
grouped together and
blocked the exit.

Jubal and I tried to run the offending dairy
product down with the condiment cart, but our
efforts didn't cut the mustard.

Then we laid down a suppressing fire of corn dogs and bombsicles.

Finally, Vera trapped the creepo carton with my Superblob 3.5 formula.

The eggnog absorbed all of the Superblob
formula and started to shake uncontrollably.
Then a huge glob of nog burst out and
transformed into a mighty hammer!

"Oh, no!" I said. "My Superblob formula has
given the eggnog the power to transform into
any object!"

"I hate when this happens," said Vera.

The eggnog blob morphed into a bat, a zombie, even a hairy tarantula, and came after the other kids.

"Stay strong, fellow students!" I yelled. "It's just taking the form of scary monsters to intimidate us! Don't be fooled!"

Then the blob transformed into the most horrifying object imaginable.

"Sweet mother of pearl!" I screamed. "It's a giant math book! Runnn!"

We were defenseless against this milky menace, and it made its escape.

CHAPTER 5

Foam for the Holidays

Later that day, at Grampa's house, the spirit of
Christmas was in the air. Grampa's hounds, Esther
and Chavez, were decorating their doghouse.

Inside, Merle was lovingly putting the finishing touches on his litter box while dancing to the *Nutcracker Suite* (meowed by an all-cat choir, of course).

Grampa was helping Gramma decorate the tree.

"Grampa!" I said. "You won't believe what happened at school today!"

"Not now, Wiley," said Grampa. "I must focus all of my concentration on supporting your Gramma. One slip and you'll have to scrape me off the floor with a spatula."

CHAPTER 6

Santa Claud

After decorating, we sat down in front of the TV.

"I tell you what," said Grampa. "There's nothing like sitting down with your loved ones and enjoying some delicious snacks and quality family Christmas entertainment."

"Oh, goody!" said Gramma. "I love Christmas movies."

"Season's greetings! This is Claud Bones, your horrible holiday host, and tonight we've got three classic yuletide yuckfests: *The Fright Before Christmas*, *The Incredible Melting Snowman*, and *I Saw a Mummy Kissing Santa Claus*. And remember, when those wintery winds have your lips feeling chapped, use melon-flavored Puckers Lip Embalmer. Preserve those suckers with Puckers!"

"I don't think so!" said Gramma. "I can't stand to see Christmas corrupted in such disgusting, slimy horror movies. I'm gonna go bake some cookies."

"Suit yourself, Granny," said Grampa. "But you'll be back. Once you hear the shrieks of the evil alien elves and the roar of Frosty 5000, the genetically mutated snowman, you'll come crawlin' back."

The movie was just starting to get good when we heard a scream from the kitchen. It was Gramma!

"Hey, hold it down in there!" said Grampa. "I can't hear the screams of the civilians with you shoutin' like that!"

"The cat's gone crazy!" screamed Gramma from the kitchen. "Merle just broke into the fridge and drank all the eggnog!"

"But that's impossible!" I said. "Merle's been out here the whole time, clawing your brand-new sofa!"

"But if it's not Merle," said Gramma, "then who is it?"

CHAPTER 7

The Spittin' Image

We peeked into the kitchen, and sure enough, there was Merle and he had plundered the fridge. At least, it looked like Merle—except he kinda looked like he was made out of gravy.

"Ooooh! How cute. A new kitty!" said Gramma.
"He looks so cuddly and...creamy!"

"That's no kitty," I said. "That's a mutant blob of
eggnog that's morphed into the shape of Merle.
We created him in school today. It looks like he's
absorbed the eggnog from the fridge."

Suddenly, the noggy feline spit a stream of goo at Gramma and swept me and Merle up into its milky tentacles!

"Oh, fiddle!" shouted Gramma. "I just cleaned this kitchen!"

Gramma was quick on the draw with her power cake mixer.

Merle held off the beast with the sign of the crazy straw (known for centuries to ward off evil eggnog).

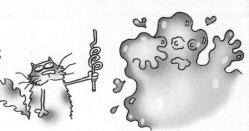

And I gave the ghastly gruel a blast of hot water from the sink.

The eggnog blob hopped to the living room and went after Grampa, but he was too wrapped up in his movie.

"Hey! Down in front!" shouted Grampa. "You're blocking the TV. I'm trying to watch Frosty eat a school bus!"

I managed to lasso the eggnog with some lights
from the Christmas tree.

"All right, Merle," I said. "Plug 'em in and stand
back!"

Merle plugged in the Christmas tree lights
and the blob lit up like a...uh, Christmas tree.
The electrified beasty quivered like a frog in a
blender, made a dash for the window, and
escaped once again.

The house was a shambles. Little pools of nog were all over the place.

"I'll run a sample of the killer nog over to Nate Farkles for analysis," I said.

"Boy!" said Grampa. "That snowman movie sure wore me out. If only real life were that exciting. I think I'm gonna hit the hay."

CHAPTER 8

The Curd on the Street

The next day, we headed to town for some more nog. The place was abuzz with activity.

"Beware, citizens!" said Cleta Van Snout. "There's an eggnog bandit on the loose. Twelve robberies just last night. I suggest you hide your nog and guard it with high-powered weaponry!"

Things were especially crazy in front of the grocery store. Cops were all over the place.

"Stay calm, folks!" said Officer Puckett. "A few moments ago this grocery store was attacked and the entire eggnog aisle was destroyed and depleted. The mayor has declared this Piggly Jiggly a disaster area and is sending in a battalion of mops and grief counselors!"

"Wait a minute! It was her!" said Luigi, the grocer, pointing at Gramma. "I saw her in the eggnog aisle before the attack!"

"That's not true!" said Gramma.

"Utterly absurd," said Grampa. "But I would like to point out that I have no idea who this woman is. I'm just here for some Pork Cracklins."

These crazy people thought Gramma was the culprit. We had to get outta there.

"Look out!" I screamed. "A runaway reindeer is headed this way!"

While the townspeople were distracted, I turned to Gramma and Grampa and shouted, "Run!"

"But I wanna see the runaway reindeer!" said Grampa.

We outran the crowd before they could identify us and stopped for a breather around the corner.

"I don't see why they think I took the eggnog," said Gramma. "Aside from crashing that blimp into the Chattanooga chimichanga factory in 1957, I've never broken the law in my life!"

"Look!" I said pointing at the big-screen TV store. "Gramma, you're on TV!"

"You saw it here first, folks," said Blue Norther.
"Actual footage of the eggnog bandit. If you see
this large, quivery woman, head for the hills!
The mayor has hired a team of local goons with
tranquilizer darts to hunt this nog-lovin' fiend
down. Have a merry Christmas."

"Oh, dear!" said Gramma.

"Don't worry, honey," said Grampa. "Those darts
might sting a little goin' in, but they won't do
any permanent damage."

"The eggnog must have morphed into Gramma to slip into the Piggly Jiggly unnoticed," I said. "We've gotta get you home before someone recognizes you. We're gonna need a disguise."

"How about Conan the Barbarian?" said Grampa. "No, I've got it—a rabid hula dancer!"

We settled on something simpler and headed home, but the town was crawling with folks looking for the bandit.

"I just hope they catch her before the school musical tonight," said Merna Figleaf. "They say there's over two hundred fifty gallons of eggnog in one of the big dance numbers. If that scoundrel shows her face tonight I'll get her in a head lock, then I'll beat her with a wet noodle. Then I'll . . ."

"Musical!" said Grampa nervously. "Heavens to Betsy! Wiley, we've gotta get you in costume. Sorry, Merna. Gotta be going."

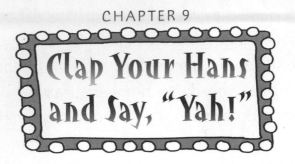

CHAPTER 9

Clap Your Hans and Say, "Yah!"

That night was the big school Christmas musical, Andrew Lloyd Webfoot's *Jingle Bell Stomp*. The play's director, Hans Lotion, and his grandson, Jurgen, greeted the crowd.

"Good evening, ladies and gentlemen."

"I know a lot of you are vorried about ze fountain of eggnog zat is ze centerpiece of my show, but do not fear. If ze eggnog bandit appears, she vill have to deal vith my army of soldiers, my vicious attack hounds, and Jurgen's beloved trained spider monkeys. Now, please, relax and enjoy ze show."

Backstage, Jubal and I were pretty nervous.

"I have a hunch that the blob will go after the eggnog sometime during the show," I said. "Probably during one of the boring musical numbers when the audience is asleep."

"I just hope no one spots your Gramma in the audience," said Jubal.

"Don't worry, Jubal," I said. "Gramma is in a brilliant disguise. No one will suspect a thing."

"I think the show is about to begin, honey—I mean, Felipe," said Grampa.

CHAPTER 10

The Quiver Dance

The show got off to a blazing start with the big-haired Sugar Sisters singing "Don't Gimme No Sass for Christmas."

Merle did some modern reindeer dance.

Then we all came out for the huge musical
number "Clog Around the Nog," where we
stomped around the fountain of eggnog.

"Hey, Wiley!" said Jubal.

"Not now, Jubal," I said. "I'm in a groove."

"But I thought you should know," said Jubal, "I
think Elvis is dancing next to me."

"That's not Elvis!" I screamed. "That's the eggnog monster!"

The blob leaped over Jubal and shot straight into the eggnog fountain.

Then it absorbed all of the nog and grew twenty times its original size! The nutmeg nightmare loomed over the audience.

"Bravo!" said Grampa. "These special effects are amazing! You'd never see this kinda thing in *Dreamgirls!*"

The soldiers, attack dogs, even the trained spider monkeys had no effect on the blob.

Hans tried to calm the audience. "It's okay, folks! Never mind ze explosions and ze shrapnel. It's all part of ze show!"

Hans turned to the blob. "Listen, you! I've vorked my tushy off on zis musical, and I vill not let it be ruined by a giant phlegmball! Ze show must go on. Sing it, girls!"

The Sugar Sisters launched into their heartfelt rendition of "Little Drummer Boy."

And a funny thing happened…

The blob exited stage right.

"Look!" I said. "The sound of the Sugar Sisters singing "Little Drummer Boy" sent the blob oozing toward the exit!"

"I'm afraid it usually has the same effect on me," said Jubal.

The stage and auditorium were utterly devastated.

"Man. The janitor's not gonna be happy about this," said Jubal.

"Vell, zat's all, folks!" said Hans. "I hope you enjoyed ze show. Please purchase a T-shirt on ze vay out, and come back next month for our presentation of *Avalanche! Ze Musical.*"

CHAPTER 11

A Grosser Look

The next morning, we went to see Nate Farkles,
Gingham's finest veterinarian, to check on the
eggnog analysis.

"Nate," I said, "did you get those samples of
eggnog I sent you?"

"I sure did," said Nate. "Thanks! They were
delicious."

"Are you telling me you drank expired, mutated, morphing eggnog?" I asked.

"I sure did," said Nate. "I used it to wash down those funny-tasting fudge balls Mrs. Logan and her Chihuahua dropped off this morn—hey, wait a minute!"

While Nate went for some mouthwash, I went into action. "Gentlemen, we've got to call a town meeting. Tonight at the school auditorium. Spread the word!"

CHAPTER 12

General Mayhem

That night, the town gathered at the school with the mayor, the police, and the military.

"Thanks for coming, folks," said two-and-a-half-star General George Gruffbelly.

"What we're dealing with here is a Blog—half blob, half eggnog—and not only is it rich and creamy and sprinkled with nutmeg, but it can take the shape of any man, woman, or overweight celebrity.

"Weapons are useless against the Blog. Only the soothing sound of "Little Drummer Boy" has any effect. Our town choir has been singing it out front for eight hours straight which has got to be unbearable for the Blog—I know it has been for me."

"Gramma," I whispered, "you don't have to wear a disguise anymore. You're safe now."

"I know," said Gramma, "but I kinda like it. I feel so mysterious and exciting."

"I can catch this beast for you," said a voice
from the back of the room. It was a looming,
creepy fellow with a candy cane hook for a
hand, a Yule log for a leg, and a posse of elves.

"Are you Santa?" asked a small boy.

"Of course not, young one," chuckled the tall
man. "I'm his second cousin, Roberto. I own
Santa's Holidaytown Shanty Village outside the
city. If you can lure the Blog to my Christmas
compound, I will capture and destroy it."

"Sounds good to me!" said Mayor Maynott. "But how will we repay you?"

"Don't be silly. I won't accept any payment," said Roberto Claus. "All I ask is that I can have your autograph. Nothing sinister going on here."

"Sure!" said the mayor, signing away.

"What charity!" said Grampa. "It warms the heart."

"I don't know," I said. "I've got a bad feeling about this."

CHAPTER 13

Dreck the Halls

Roberto Claus took us on a free tour of Santa's Holidaytown Shanty Village.

"Wow!" I said. "You've got a whole lagoon made of eggnog. Aren't you worried about a Blog attack?"

"I'm counting on one, my boy!" said Roberto.

"Follow me," he said as we strolled through his enormous gift shop. "Step into my gingerbread trolley and I'll show you wonders that will make your spine tingle, your nostrils flare, and your heart glow like a lightning bug's fanny."

"Must be some trolley!" said Grampa.

Roberto took us on a first-class tour of his Christmas paradise.

"Wow!" said Jubal. "You have your own cows!"

"That's right," said Roberto. "And their udders are filled not with milk, but with pure, glistening eggnog."

"Sounds disgustingly delicious!" said Grampa.

"Here you'll find my killer snow-bots," said Roberto. "And over there is Crumby, the fruitcake monster."

"Ugh!" I said. "I hate fruitcake!"

"I wouldn't say that too loud. Crumby might squash you like a ripe kumquat!" said Roberto as we finished the tour. "So that's it, folks. If you can lure the Blog to my eggnog extravaganza, I'll use everything in my arsenal to destroy it."

CHAPTER 14

Use Your Noggin

So we strapped a loudspeaker onto the car and drove through Gingham County spreading the word about Roberto's Christmas wonderland.

"Come on down, folks!" I yelled. "Come see the world's largest supply of eggnog! Bring the kids. Bring your camera. Bring your aunt Brenda!"

Hopefully, my announcement would lure the sinister slime.

CHAPTER 15

Something Liquid This Way Comes

That night we set up a stakeout in front of the eggnog lagoon, and we waited...and waited.

"Roberto," I said. "What's it like at the North Pole?"

"The North Pole," said Roberto. "People think it's all sugarplums and candy canes....

"No one ever mentions the cyborg polar bears, like the one that took my hand.

"Or the clan of Siberian snow orcs that waged war on Santa's village for one hundred years.

"Or the evil snow wizard, Barnabus Ice Beard—a man so dastardly, he was known to rob the poor, use kittens for handkerchiefs, and cheat on book reports."

"Boy!" said Grampa. "You sure never hear about that stuff in any of those Christmas songs."

Suddenly, we got a transmission over the walkie-talkie: "This is agent Cold Turkey. Come in!"

I responded quickly. "We hear you loud and clear, Cold Turkey! What's goin' on?"

Cold Turkey was the code name for Gramma, and boy was she getting into the whole disguise thing.

"I've spotted the Blog!" said Gramma. "He's heading toward you from the south. I repeat, the Blog is coming your way. Over and out!"

CHAPTER 16

As the Milk Turns

The Blog approached us in the shape of a giant bag of Pork Cracklins. Grampa couldn't resist.

"Must have Cracklins!" said Grampa as he marched toward the beast, mesmerized.

"Yikes!" I yelled. "It's got Grampa! Quick! Roberto, release your fruitcake monster and killer snowmen to destroy the Blog!"

"Actually," said Roberto, "I've changed my mind. Come on in, my drippy friend! Take a dip in my eggnog lagoon!"

The Blog plunged into the lagoon and absorbed all of the eggnog.

"You dirty dog!" I yelled. "You tricked us!"

The Blog grew to outrageous proportions.

"Now my arsenal of Christmas supermonsters is complete!" yelled Roberto as he pulled out a megaphone. "Citizens of Gingham County, you have five minutes to evacuate. I'm taking over this town!"

"You'd expect better from a seven-foot-tall creepy dude with a candy cane hook for a hand who hangs with elves," said Grampa.

"This is outrageous!" screamed the mayor. "You can't just kick us out of our own town!"

"Of course I can!" said Roberto. "It's all perfectly legal according to this contract that you 'autographed.' It says that if I capture the Blog, you turn all of Gingham County over to me."

"Rats!" said the mayor. "I've gotta quit signing these things!"

"This Roberto guy makes the Grinch look like Mary Poppins," said Grampa.

"But why?" I asked. "Why do you need Gingham County?"

"Because I'm tired of that do-gooder, Santa, getting all the attention," said Roberto. "I will create a Christmas empire that will put the North Pole to shame. I will deliver toys and ugly sweaters to the children of the world. And when Santa tries to challenge me, I will defeat him with my army of elves, fruitcake monsters, and mutating eggnog. It will be glorious!"

"I think this guy's a couple beans short of a burrito," said Grampa.

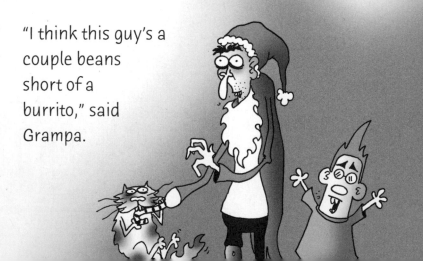

CHAPTER 17

Noggy By Nature

"Oops!" said Roberto. "Your time is up. I'll have to evacuate you myself. Christmas critters, attack!"

"Well, this it it, boys," said Grampa. "Stomped by a giant fruitcake. Why couldn't it have been a giant German chocolate cake with extra frosting?"

The attack was on! Merle and I dodged the
super nasal carrot rockets of the killer snowbots
with our amazing shaolin moves.

Unfortunately, Jubal was no match for the elves
and their fake snow-flocking devices.

General Gruffbelly showed up with tanks, but expected a blog, not a bunny.

"Hold your fire, gentlemen," he said. "I will not fire upon a cuddly, fluffy bunny. Not on my watch!"

Of course, the bunny attacked mercilessly.

"I guess that's why he's only a two-and-a-half-star general," said Grampa.

CHAPTER 18

Who Let the Nog Out?

We formed a barrier, and Roberto attacked with his elves, armed with cheese ball-lobbing catapults.

"Arm yourselves, citizens!" shouted Grampa. "Let this day be known as Eggnog Independence Day!"

"Or Soggy Noggy Bloggy Day." said the mayor.

"How about Nate Farkles Day?" said Nate Farkles.

But their conversation was cut short when a
giant nut-covered cheese ball landed on Grampa.

"Grampa!" I yelled. "Are you okay?"

"Wiley, my boy," gasped Grampa, "I just have one
final wish: can somebody bring me some crack-
ers? This cheese is delicious!"

Just then, a wave of eggnog crashed over us.

"This is just awful!" said the mayor. "And to think it's only two hours until Christmas!"

"Two hours?" said Grampa. "I guess I'd better start my Christmas shopping!"

"Don't worry," I said, pulling out my walkie-talkie. "All right, Gramma. Operation Super Absorbent is in effect!"

CHAPTER 19

Sponge Blob, Square Pan

Suddenly, the Blog came to a screeching halt.
There, in front of us, was Gramma's car, and it
was blasting Christmas music out of the
loudspeaker on the roof.

"Hey, Blog!" said Gramma. "I'm feelin' a little dairy intolerant! Sing it, girls!"

The car was loaded up with the big-hair Sugar Sisters and several of Gramma's elderly friends, and they launched into an extra-special version of "Little Drummer Boy."

The caroling car forced the Blog right up to the edge of Lookout, Gingham's most convenient cliff. The girls sang one last chorus of "Ba-rump-bum-bum-bum" with gusto, and it drove the Blog over the edge.

The Blog plummeted hundreds of feet, but since it was a Blog it really wasn't damaged when it hit the ground.

But little did it realize that it had landed not on the ground, but on the world's largest sponge cake. Vera had been doing some serious baking, and her giant cake absorbed the helpless Blog.

The pigeons devoured that sponge cake in no time. It was a horrible sight.

"Oh, I can't watch!" said Gramma.

"I know, honey," said Grampa. "It's a weird and disturbing sight. Yet somehow I can't tear my eyes away from it. It's like watching an episode of *The Wiggles*."

CHAPTER 20

A Crumby Ending

We carried the drained and expired eggnog carton and put it in its proper recycling bin.

"I'm gonna miss that little stinker," said Grampa. "He sure was rotten, but he had a lot of guts."

"Crumbs!" yelled Roberto. "All that's left of my beautiful Blog are a few measly crumbs! Well, I'm not done with Gingham County yet."

"You still have to deal with Crumby, the fruitcake monster! If you think you hate fruitcake now, wait until Crumby gets through with you."

"Actually, we like fruitcake," came a sweet, angelic voice out of the blue.

It was the Sugar Sisters. "We love the tough leathery texture of fruitcake and the mysterious sugar-soaked fruit particles."

"They like me," said Crumby. "Nobody likes fruitcake. Crumby gonna cry." The Sugar Sisters gave Crumby a hug.

"I've gotta get some meaner monsters," said Roberto.

While Crumby made some new friends, Merle took care of the killer snowbots with a monkey wrench.

"Ohhh!" Roberto wailed. "My plan is ruined! What else could possibly go wrong?"

Suddenly, the elves got nervous and a strange sound filled the night air.

"Is that the sound of sleigh bells?" asked Jubal.

"It sounds more like the revving of motorcycles to me," I said.

"Nooooo!" screamed Roberto. "He's found me!"

CHAPTER 21

High on a Hog

It was Santa! The real Santa Claus! And he was riding a motorcycle. He landed right in front of us.

"Wow!" I said. "I always figured he'd be riding in a sleigh."

"Of course not," said Grampa. "Santa traded in his sleigh for a chopper years ago. I saw it on CNN" (that's the **C**hristmas **N**ews **N**etwork).

"Roberto," said Santa, shaking his finger, "did you get out of your padded room again?"

Roberto looked very guilty, "Yes, sir. I just get so bored and so cold up there at the North Pole."

"Let's go, Roberto," said Santa. "I'm taking you back home to Santa's Institute for Holiday Nuts."

"You never let me have any fun!" said Roberto as he climbed into a peppermint paddy wagon.

"Sorry about my cousin, folks," said Santa. "Sometimes he just gets these wild ideas."

"It's all right," said Grampa. "I'm sure he meant well when he clobbered me with a giant cheese ball and flooded the town with rancid eggnog."

"I think I know how you can repay us, big guy," I said. "How 'bout a quick spin on your flying hog?"

"Welllll," Santa said, "okay. But we gotta make it fast. I've got five billion presents to deliver, and my back is killing me."

Santa gave us a first-class flight over Gingham County, and it was awesome.

"Everything looks so small from up here," said Grampa. "Hey, look! I can see your gramma. No, wait! That's just a Volkswagen."

"I heard that!" yelled Gramma.

Well, that's my Christmas story, folks. Hans added Crumby to the Christmas musical. His version of "Puttin' on the Ritz" brought down the house.

The unruly elves were entered into a five-step elf help program. They are making tremendous progress.

Gramma served up a delicious Christmas dinner of honey-slathered ham with all the fixins'— except eggnog, of course.

And as for those pigeons that ate the mutant eggnog, scientists have assured us that there were no side effects and everything is okay.

That's right. There's absolutely nothing to worry about. Everything is 100% A-OK, peachy keen, hunky-dory.

Gramma just printed up a batch of lovely
homemade Christmas cards, but something
went wrong with her printer. One of these cards
just ain't right. Pick out the differences before
she takes them to the post office.

The answers are on the back. Anyone caught cheating has to gargle eggnog for five minutes!